CLUNKY
And His Happy-O-Metre

For Reuben, Jude, Caleb and Jaiden.
Fill up your tanks every day x x x

CLUNKY

And His Happy-O-Metre

If you walk down the winding lane,
And up the stony path,

You'll find Clunky the Robot,
Who sleeps in an old tin bath.

Clunky lives with robot parents,
And his sister Clinky too,

But the friend he really loves the most
Is his robo-dog Choo Choo!

Grey nuts and bolts and metal limbs
Make up our robot friend,

He glides so well and oils so much
He rarely needs a mend.

But every now and then, you see,
He'll need a little tweak,

His happy-o-metre drops to red
And all he can do is squeak.

"Well what's a happy-o-metre?"
I hear your cry resound.
Just look inside each robot
And there's a tank that can be found.

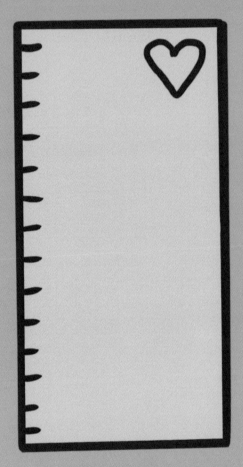

It has a little heart shape,
In the corner; can you see?
We like this tank to stay full,
But sometimes it's empty as can be!

Each day Clunky checks his little tank
When he wakes up from his sleep,
A full green heart shows a happy tank,
And he makes a grateful beep.

But some days it's only half full
And a yellow heart is shown,
And on the worst of all days
Only red is in the zone.

Clunky wakes up from his sleep
On one cold winter's morn,
He's grumpy and he's tired,
His heart feels a bit torn.

He had a bad night's sleep,
With one big scary dream,

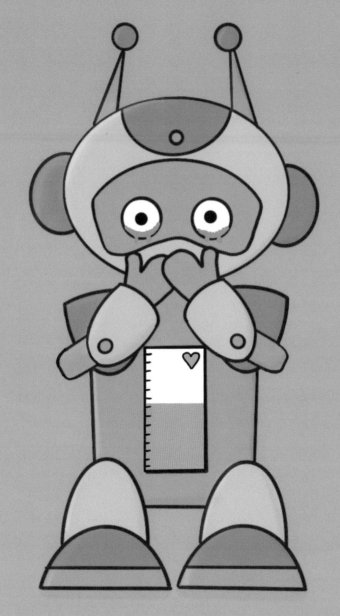

And he checks his happy-o-metre,
Then lets out a little scream.

His tank is down to yellow,
That's a warning sign for sure,
His horrible sleep and scary dream
Have left him needing more.

Clunky needs to fill his tank up fast,
He can't let it drain to red,
Quick as a flash he gets up,
gets washed,
And makes his old tin bed.

Clunky dashes to the kitchen
Where Mum, Dad and Clinky sit,
They're eating toast and cereal,
And even a banana split!

"Mum, Dad, my tank is down to yellow!
Help! I need a top up fast!"
His Mum gives him a long, tight hug
And he feels some warmth at last.

Clunky goes out to the park with friends,
He runs and jumps and skips,
The happy-o-metre fills up once more,
In squirts and bursts and drips.

But then Clunky falls down and cries,
He's hurt his arm - oh no!

The pain and tears make him sad,
And his tank gets a little low.

His friends all run to pick him up,
They care and make Clunky smile,

He soon forgets his painful arm
And slides and swings for a while.

Playing, running and laughing with friends,
All fill his tank to the brim,

But sadness and hurt, being tired
or scared,
Make Clunky feel quite grim.

A walk with Choo Choo and a chat with Nan

All fill up his tank a bit more,

At bedtime he smiles - his tank is on green;
Clunky drifts off with a loud snore.

Everyone you will ever meet
Has a tank they need to care for,

Mums and Dads, uncles and aunts,
Boys and girls, people galore.

How is your heart feeling today? Is it green?

Or yellow?

Or red?

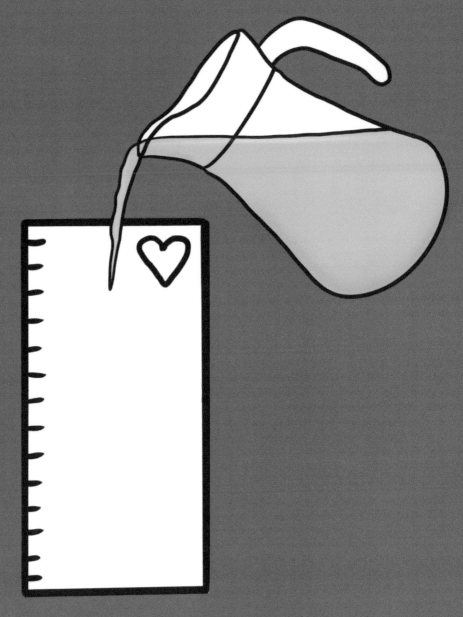

What can you do to top up your tank
Before you get back into bed?

Spend time with friends,

Eat yummy food,

Ride your bike to the lake,

Watch your favourite show,

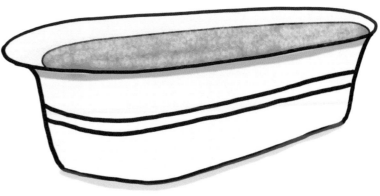

Have a warm bath,

Or bake a chocolate cake.

Remember to always check your tank,

Morning, noon and night,

Look after yourself, you are important,
Make your green light shine bright!

Note to Grown Ups

Self-care is such an important topic to introduce to young children. Using an imaginary tank in our bodies can help them to understand how our tank can fill up, but also how it can be drained.

Spend some time helping your child identify what fills and drains their tank, and also allow them to see you putting in the time to fill up your tank too. Creating these habits from a young age will help nurture your child's mental health as they grow up.

Printed in Great Britain
by Amazon

81083705R00022